THIS WALKER BOOK BELONGS TO:

_____

_____

_____

_____

To Lucienne
L. H.

First published 1995
by Walker Books Ltd
87 Vauxhall Walk, London SE11 5HJ

This edition published 2001

2 4 6 8 10 9 7 5 3 1

Text © 1995 Martin Waddell
Illustrations © 1995 Leo Hartas

The right of Martin Waddell to be identified as author
of this work has been asserted by him in accordance
with the Copyright, Designs and Patents Act 1988

Printed in Hong Kong

British Library Cataloguing in Publication Data:
a catalogue record for this book
is available from the British Library

ISBN 0-7445-8275-X

Mimi
and the
Picnic

Written by
MARTIN WADDELL
Illustrated by
LEO HARTAS

WALKER BOOKS
AND SUBSIDIARIES
LONDON · BOSTON · SYDNEY

Mimi lived with her mouse sisters
and brothers beneath the big tree.
The mice came in all sizes, but the
smallest of all was called Hugo.

One day they all went for a picnic
on the bank of the river.

Mimi laid out the tea for her
sisters and brothers.

Hugo sat on his Big Leaf and
watched her, while the sisters
and brothers ran off to play.

They played …   and they played …

and they played …

and they played …

and they played … and they played.

But when they came back for their tea, Hugo's Big Leaf was empty. There was no sign of Hugo at all!

"Hugo's so small he'd be easily lost," Mimi said. "We'd better start looking for Hugo at once."

The mouse sisters and brothers scuttled about, under the leaves and round Robin's Nest and up Badger's Path by the two Rusty Tins and down by Mole's Hole.

"Hugo's so small we can't find him at all,"
the mouse sisters and brothers told Mimi.
"Try looking some more!" Mimi said.

And they looked ...   and they looked ...

and they looked ...

and they looked …

and they looked.

And then they looked a lot more – some of them looked where they'd looked before! "Hugo's lost," Mimi said.

The sisters and brothers and Mimi were very upset. Hugo was *so* small and all of them loved him a lot.

Mimi sat down on Hugo's Big Leaf and started to cry.
Great big mouse tears rolled down her cheeks, and her mouse sisters and brothers cried too, for they all loved little Hugo so much.

They cried …   and they cried …

and they cried …

and they cried …

and they cried …

AND THEN…

They found Hugo, but he
wasn't as small as before …

for he'd had a *very* big tea!

MARTIN WADDELL says of *Mimi and the Picnic*, "Hugo is the star of this story, for me. The idea of the little mouse eating and getting fatter and fatter and fatter while everyone else searched for him was too good to resist."

Martin Waddell is widely regarded as one of the finest contemporary writers of books for young people. Twice Winner of the Smarties Book Prize – for *Farmer Duck* and *Can't You Sleep, Little Bear?* – he also won the Kurt Maschler Award for *The Park in the Dark* and the Best Books for Babies Award for *Rosie's Babies*. Among his many other titles are *Owl Babies*; *Night Night, Cuddly Bear* and three other stories about Mimi. He was the Irish nominee for the 2000 Hans Christian Andersen Award. He lives with his wife Rosaleen in County Down, Northern Ireland.

LEO HARTAS says, "Trifle! In order to paint the trifle in the book, I had to paint from a real one and it took a fair bit of time. I remember eating rather too much trifle when really I should have been painting it."

Leo Hartas has illustrated over twenty books, including the three other Mimi stories. He taught himself computer graphics and animation and now has a small company working on new ideas for interactive television and the Internet. Of his work he says, "All I have ever done has been because I enjoy it but I'm delighted to find children enjoy it too!" Leo lives in Brighton with his wife and three children.

Other Mimi stories by Martin Waddell and Leo Hartas

Mimi and the Dream House   0-7445-8274-1 (p/b) £3.99
Mimi and the Blackberry Pies   0-7445-8279-2 (p/b) £3.99
Mimi's Christmas   0-7445-7213-4 (p/b) £4.99